All About Me!

by JOAN WALSH ANGLUND

with EMILY ANGLUND-NELLEN

SCHOLASTIC INC.

New York Toronto London Auckland Sydney

ISBN 0-590-33809-9

12 11 10 9 8 7 6 5 4 3 2 1   9   6 7 8 9/8 0 1/9

Printed in the U.S.A.   10

All About Me!

No two people are quite alike...
Surely we all know that's true.
No one will ever be quite like "me"
As no one else can be "you."

I am the only one who sees
the World from my own Special View.
So I've gathered these things
That are All about Me

...and I'll keep them
my whole life
through!

Every person's different
no two are quite the same.
So let me introduce myself
... to start with,
... Here's my NAME!

Write your signature here.

MY NAME IS

Mirror, Mirror,
...on the Wall,
who's the Very Best
of them all?

People come in various forms,
... in every shape and size.

Here is what I look like,

...my face

Round	
Square	
Oval	
Pointed	
Other	

... my nose

Upturned	
Large	
Small	
Long	
Short	
Broken	
Strong	

... my eyes!

Blue	
Brown	
Gray	
Green	
Other	

(Check one of each.)

Wavy   Straight   Braids   Long   Curly   Short

My hair is

Snip a piece
and put it
here.

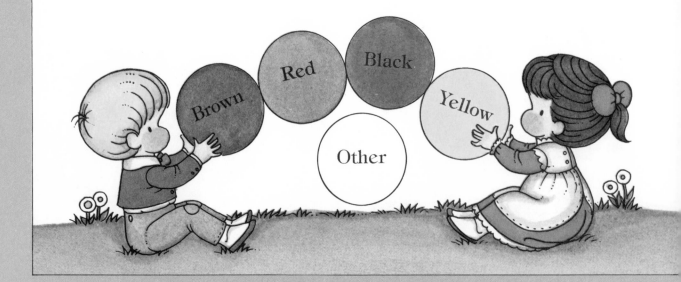

A Self Portrait

this is a picture of me...
I drew it myself

I weigh _____

and "watching" it.

I am _____ tall

...and still "growing."

My Hobbies

....

....

....

....

....

....

....

My
Favorite
Hobby

this is my Hand-print....

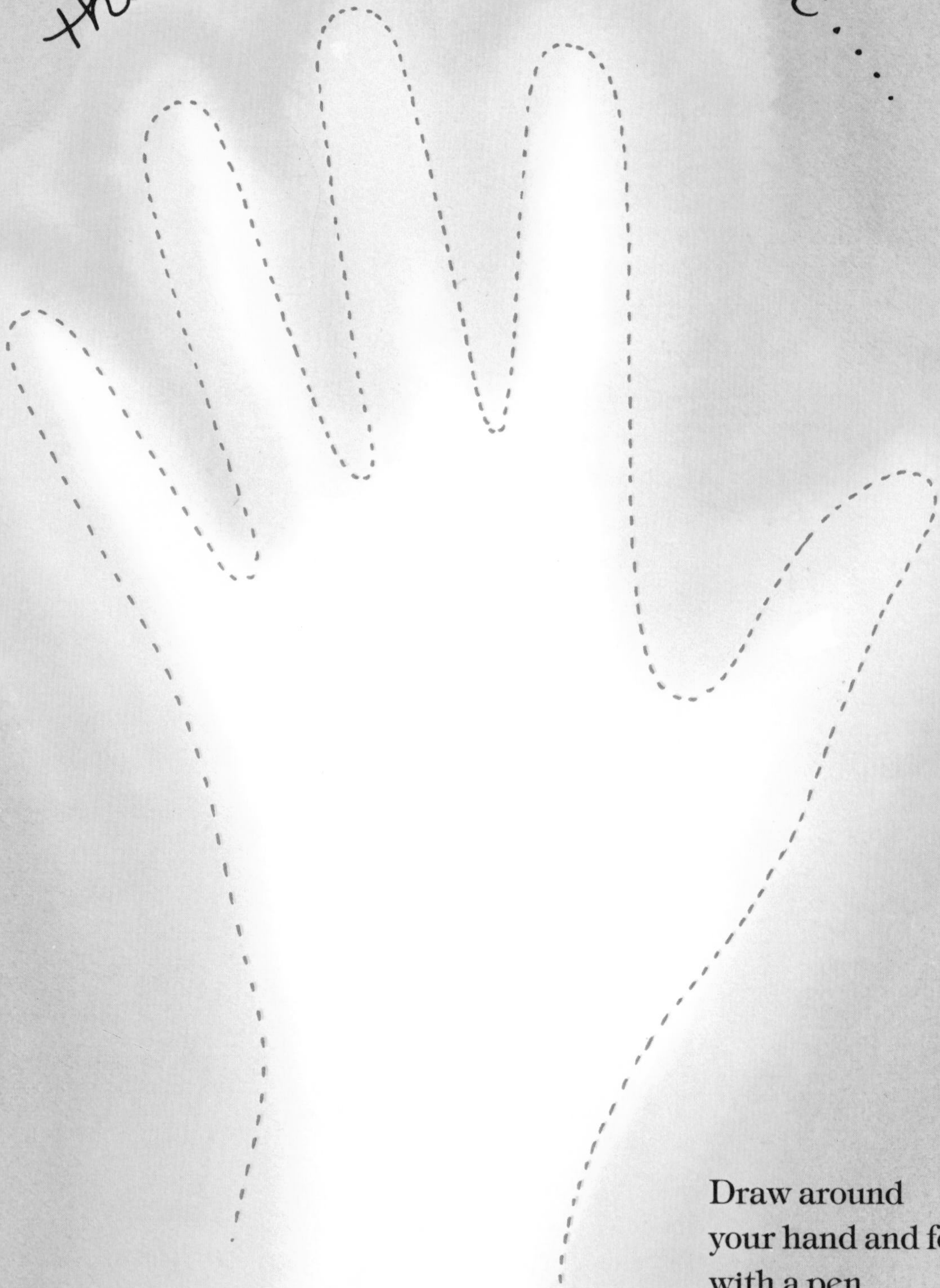

Date

_____

_____

Draw around
your hand and foot
with a pen
and color them
in with crayons.

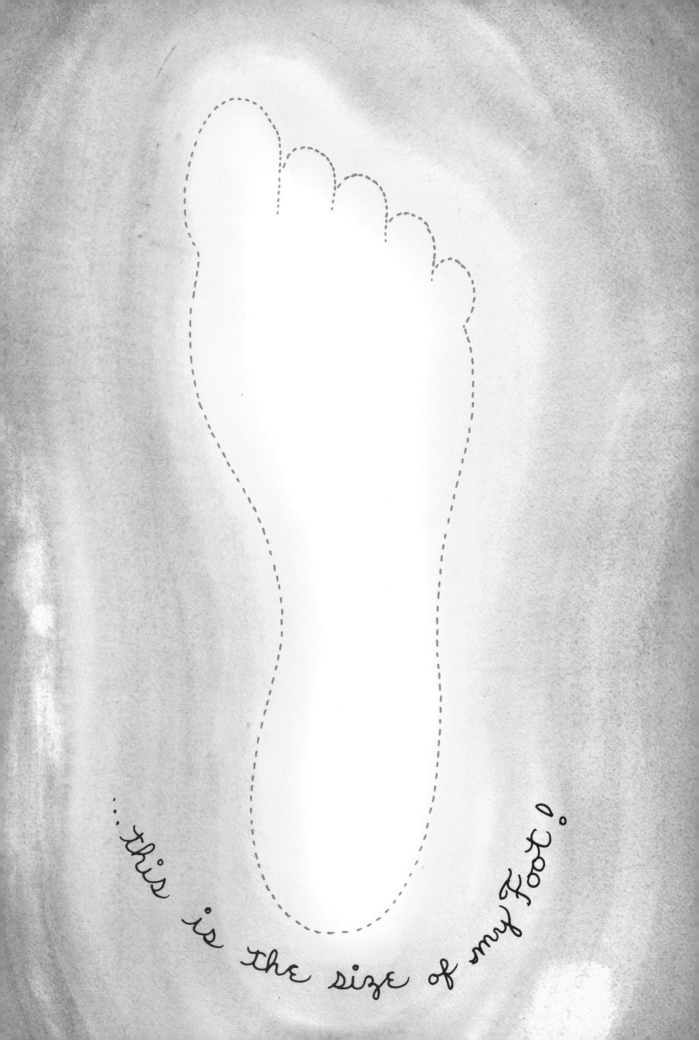

...this is the size of my Foot!

My Age is

....

My Birthday is

....

Put the candles on the cake.

Draw and color the right number
of candles.

Birthday Present

Draw a picture of your birthday present inside this package.

Especially for me

For my next birthday I would like
to get a

....

I was Born
in ....
(place)

at .... on ....
(time)   (day of the week) (date) (year)

They dressed me in ....
(Color in pink or blue.)

I weighed ....
(lbs. & oz.)

and was .... long!
(inches)

Hello World!

The Zodiac

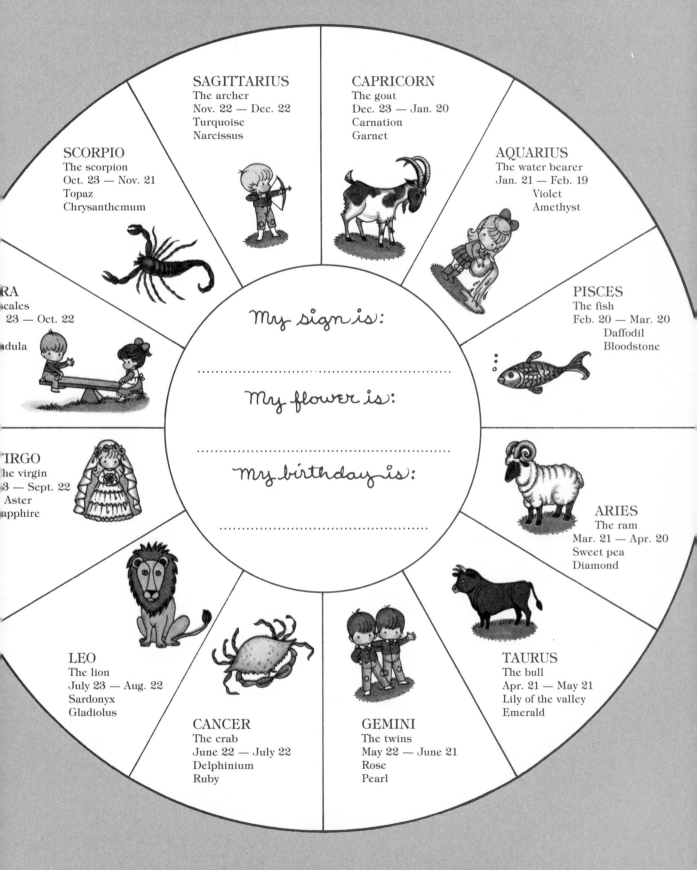

SAGITTARIUS
The archer
Nov. 22 — Dec. 22
Turquoise
Narcissus

CAPRICORN
The goat
Dec. 23 — Jan. 20
Carnation
Garnet

SCORPIO
The scorpion
Oct. 23 — Nov. 21
Topaz
Chrysanthemum

AQUARIUS
The water bearer
Jan. 21 — Feb. 19
Violet
Amethyst

..RA
..scales
..23 — Oct. 22
..dula

PISCES
The fish
Feb. 20 — Mar. 20
Daffodil
Bloodstone

..IRGO
..he virgin
..3 — Sept. 22
..Aster
..apphire

ARIES
The ram
Mar. 21 — Apr. 20
Sweet pea
Diamond

LEO
The lion
July 23 — Aug. 22
Sardonyx
Gladiolus

TAURUS
The bull
Apr. 21 — May 21
Lily of the valley
Emerald

CANCER
The crab
June 22 — July 22
Delphinium
Ruby

GEMINI
The twins
May 22 — June 21
Rose
Pearl

My sign is:
....

My flower is:
....

My birthday is:
....

My Special Traits

Check which trait suits you best.
☐ Use square

I am Loud.
I love attention.
☐

I am Quiet.
I am very shy.
☐

I am Cautious.
I'd rather be safe
than sorry.
☐

I am Daring.
I take chances.
☐

I am a Loner.
I like privacy.
☐

I am Friendly.
I love a crowd.
☐

I am Lazy.
Bed suits me
best.
☐

I am very Active.
Let's go jogging.
☐

Interesting Facts About Me

Check which describes you best.

I do ☐
I do not ☐ wear glasses.

I do ☐
I do not ☐ have braces.

I am ☐ right-handed.
☐ left-handed.

I do ☐
I do not ☐ have dimples.

I do ☐
I do not ☐ have long eyelashes.

I do ☐
I do not ☐ have freckles.

☐ I have a big temper.
☐ I am easy-going.

☐ I always try to help others.
☐ I am usually too busy to bother.

☐ I have a good sense of humor.
☐ I don't get jokes.

☐ I am very neat and organized.
☐ I'm messy…but lovable.

☐ I have a good singing voice.
☐ I can't carry a tune.

☐ I am a day person.
☐ I am a night person.

These are the things I collect

....
....
....
....
....

Clubs I belong to

....
....

Awards ☆ Honors ☆ Prizes
I have received

....
....

Sports I've participated in

....
....

Write to me
at this Address

zip

hello
you can call me
at this number.

① ☐

② ☐ *Little House*

A HOUSE IN the SUBURBS IS BEST FOR ME!

I LIVE IN A LITTLE COTTAGE BY THE SHORE

Big House

Home is where the Heart is!

My Home looks like number ☐

⑦ ☐

OUR HOME IS "DOWN ON THE FARM!"

Country House

these are M

My favorite name

....

My favorite sport

....

My favorite team

....

My favorite type of clothes

....

My favorite song

....

My favorite musical group

....

My favorite type of food

....

My favorite type of drink

....

My favorite flower

....

FAVORITE things!

My favorite book
....

My favorite animal
....

My favorite movie
....

My favorite movie star
....

My favorite month of the year
....

My favorite place in the world
....

My favorite recreation
....

My favorite President
....

My favorite tv show
....

My favorite day of the week
....

My favorite holiday
....

My favorite person who ever lived
....

My Family

Grandfather

Grandmother

Your
Father

Uncles

Aunts

or
Cousins

Your
Brothers

Me

PAINTS

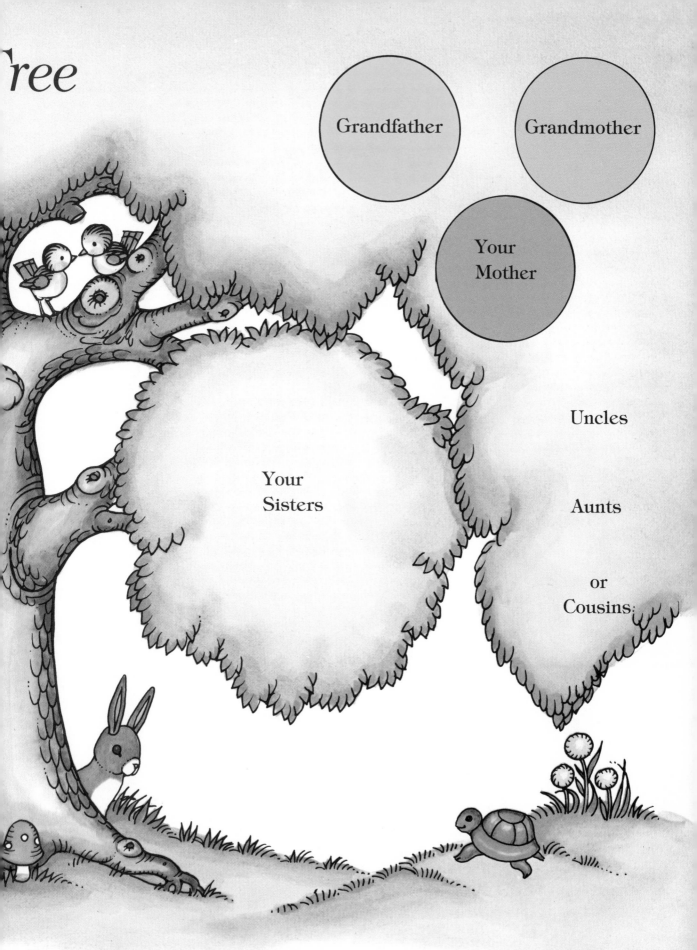

ree

Grandfather

Grandmother

Your
Mother

Uncles

Aunts

or
Cousins

Your
Sisters

Paste in photos of your family in proper places
and write in their names.

My FRIENDS ♡

"A friend is a present we give ourselves."

R.L. STEVENSON

My oldest friend

....

My youngest friend

....

My tallest friend

....

My shortest friend

....

My funniest friend

....

My very BEST FRIEND

....

EVERYTHING is HAPPIER when SHARED with a FRIEND!

Pets

A Pet can be a
very special friend

Pets I have had

....

....

....

Pets I would like
to have someday.

....

....

....

The First Times

My first memory

....

My first home

....

My first friend's name

....

My first day at school

....

My first teacher's name

....

My first public performance

....

The first time I won something

....

The Worst Times

The biggest mistake I ever made

....

My most embarrassing moment

....

The worst grade I ever got

....

The meanest thing I've ever done

....

The saddest day of my life

....

The Best Times

The best party I ever went to

....

The kindest thing I've ever
done...

....

The happiest day
of my life...

....

The bravest thing
I've ever done...

....

Some things I'd like to do someday

....

....

....

When I grow up I want to be

....

....

The things I think are the most important in life

....

....

Secrets

Some things no one else knows about me

....

....

....

My best quality

....

My worst fault

....

Things about me I want to change

....

....

....

Memories

this is me! ...Everyday...

Paste in
photos.

...on Special Occasions!

Paste in
photos.

and
Good Times

...with Good Friends

Paste in
photos
and souvenirs.

Though Time goes by
...we'll always remember!

PLACES
I have been...

PLACES
I have yet to see

my SCHOOL DAZE

My grade is: 1 2 3 4 5 6 7 8 9 10 (Circle one.)

My teachers' names are   (Put a star next to your favorite.)

....

....

My favorite subject is   (Fill in the square next to your favorite.)

Math ☐   Reading ☐

Art ☐   Music ☐

Gym ☐   Spelling ☐

History ☐   Science ☐

Writing ☐   Computers ☐

Recess ☐

IT TAKES
A HEAP of LEARNING
TO MAKE A KID
A GRADUATE.

SCHOOL

School is where we go
To learn all the things
we'll probably forget by the time
we grow up

I go to .... school.

On a scale from 1 to 10, I rate it a ....

I leave for school at ....

I get home from school by ....

I go to school by Bus ○   Pogo stick ○
                   Car ○   Roller skate ○
                   Bike ○   Skate board ○
               I walk ○   Other ....

(Color in one circle.)

As a student
I am
Very good ☐
Sort of good ☐
Not so bad ☐
Terrible ☐
(Check one.)

I JUST GET USED TO VACATION... AND IT'S TIME TO START SCHOOL AGAIN!

Yes!

Things about which
I'm proud

....
....
....
....
....
....

No!

Things about which
I'm sorry

....
....
....
....
....
....

Good Resolutions

I promise to ....

....
....
....

Goals I'd like to achieve

....
....
....
....

Famous Last Words

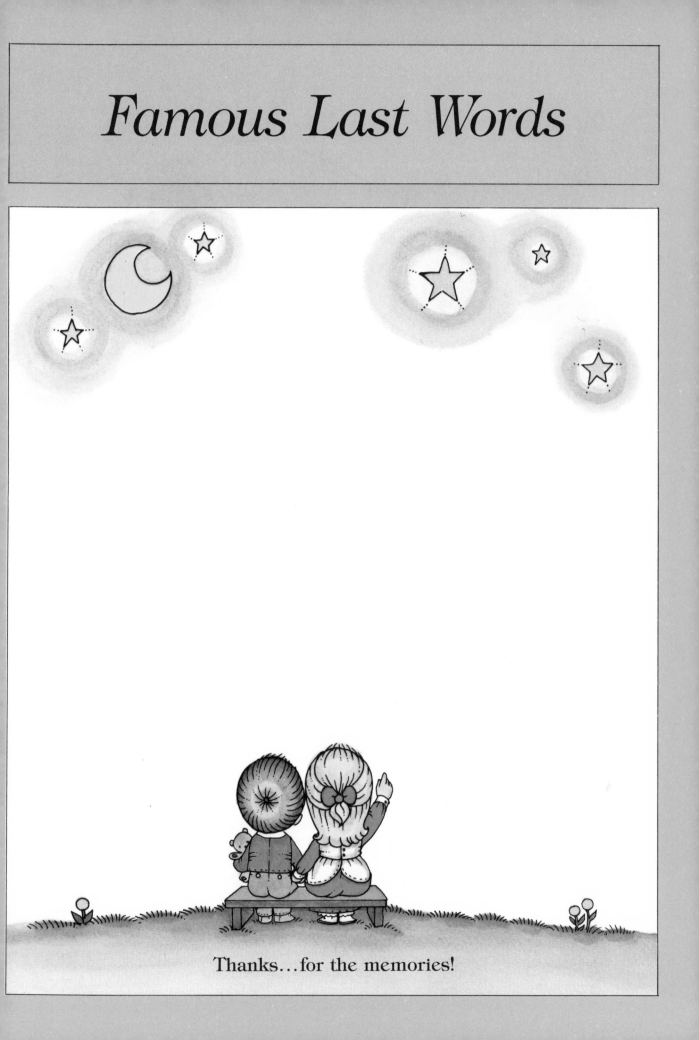

Thanks...for the memories!

I've written this book
    ... All about me
So I can keep
        each dear memory,

Each hope that I've had
    Each good time, and friend,

And now that I've finished
    it all ... at the end,

I'll keep it forever... so safely,
        ... you'll see!

'cause this is MY story!
    ... it's
        All about Me!

signed ....   date ....

⭐

                                        year ....